Cuffing In the Summer: A Charleston Fling

By: Britt Renee

Synopsis

Roneshia aka RiRi is a sixteen-year-old high school student who's had her share of troubles just being a teenager. Her and her mother are desperately trying to make ends meet with her being an only child. Her father is a functioning alcoholic who doesn't hesitate to violently show how he feels. When school is out for the summer, RiRi wants to just work and focus on trying to get her and her mother out of the situation they're in. She doesn't care about the upcoming parties or the latest fashions; she just wants them to be free.

Jay is new in town. He's an upcoming boss in the streets and his name rings bells everywhere he goes. The only problem with him is his friends with benefits, Tisha, who believes that they have more than just a sexual relationship. He meets RiRi and instantly falls for her and vows to make her his. With street beefs looming and Tisha in the background wanting to fight for what she believes is hers, Jay will have to make sure he lives through the summer to be able to claim his newfound love interest. Let's take this ride with RiRi and Jay and hope that love will prevail!!

RiRi

Tomorrow is the last day of school and I couldn't be more happy. This school year at R.B. Stall High School has been the year from hell. I had to deal with all the petty bitches that didn't like me for whatever reason and I couldn't care less. But when they stepped to me about niggas I didn't even know was looking at me then it became a problem.

I wasn't fighting over no nigga I didn't know or want to get to know but I was gonna bust they shit for stepping to me like some punk bitch, especially when I asked them to nicely get out of my face. I was already going through the regular teasing of being one of the few people that didn't have it like that to always get the new name brand shit that had just come out and personally I didn't care. I was just a regular 16-year-old trying to live my life.

As the last bell rang, I hurriedly grabbed my books and backpack so that I could go. I ran out of my classroom and headed to the bus loop so that I could see my bus.

"RiRi, wait up!!" I rolled my eyes at the voice and hurriedly kept walking as if I didn't hear her while looking for my school bus. "RiRi, you ain't hear me," Dominique said as she got closer.

"Yeah, I'm just tryna hurry up and get on this bus so I can go home," I said.

"Oh, my bad, are you coming to school tomorrow?" she asked.

"I don't know. I don't really want to, but I guess I'll have to see what my mama says," I told her as I located my bus.

"Okay, well, umm text me later," she said as she walked away to find her bus.

I wasn't trying to be mean but I just wanted to get home. She was one of the few people that still was a real friend to me and didn't switch up on me when all these hating ass bitches started talking about me in school.

I found my seat, put on my headphones and listened to music until we got to my bus stop. Once there, I got off the bus and walked home which was about five minutes away from the stop. When I got in the house, I went to my room to take out my work clothes and to charge my phone. I had just gotten a job at Burger King about a week ago and was excited about my new job. I went in the bathroom to shower and wash the day off of me so that I could be ready once my mama pulled up.

After my shower, I went back to my room and got ready. Just as I was finishing up, my mama blew the horn from outside. I looked around glad that I cleaned up before school this morning. I didn't want her fussing about the house and she had just gotten off of her first job. I went outside and locked the front door and got in the car with my mama.

"Hey, mama, how was your day?" I asked as I kissed her on the cheek.

"It was okay, baby, thank you for asking. How was your day at school?" she said.

"It was okay. I'm just ready for it to be over. Oh, and here, I got my report card today so I don't have to go tomorrow," I told her all in one breath as I handed her the report card. She kept driving and smiled.

"Okay, baby, as long as you passed you can stay home tomorrow," she said as I laughed.

"Mama they ain't doing nothing tomorrow anyway except breaking up fights so even if I failed I wouldn't learn anything tomorrow," I said as she laughed at me.

"That is so true," she said. We continued to talk as she drove and when we pulled up to Burger King I got out the car and gave my mama a kiss on the cheek and told her I loved her.

"Ma make sure you rest okay. The house is clean and you don't have to cook tonight. I'll eat at work, I love you," I told her.

"Okay baby, I love you too," she said. Knowing her she'd find something to do while I was at work. Once she drove off, I went inside and prepared to get something to eat since I was two hours early. Unfortunately for me, they were short-handed and my manager asked me to clock in early. I said okay and went ahead and clocked in. I helped out on the back line while the orders were coming in. Luckily, when I started training last week when the front was slow I went in the back and learned how they were doing everything so that I could help anytime we needed it.

After about four hours, I finally was able to take a much-needed break. My manager gave me a free meal since I helped out so I took that and went in the lobby and texted my mama to check on her and listen to music as I ate my food. I suddenly felt someone standing over me and looked up and there was this cute ass guy there with the most gorgeous dark brown eyes I've ever seen. His eyes were naturally glossy and he was dark skinned with a low cut and looked to be almost 6 feet tall. I removed my headphones when I noticed him talking.

"So you just gonna sit out here and eat while me and my people waiting for somebody to take our fuckin order?!!!" he demanded.

"Excuse me," I said with an apparent attitude.

"Ain't no excuse me. We been standing up front and nobody up here, and I saw you walk from back there when we was getting out the car and then you come out here and eat. So why ain't nobody taking our orders?" he said with more attitude.

By then, I had done forgotten how cute I had just thought he was because of his ugly ass attitude.

"First of all, I am on break. Second of all, there should be someone up front right now. You could've called out for a manager if that was the case," I told him sternly.

"Yeah, okay, well I want the manager," he said.

I huffed and wrapped up my food and stood up to go and get the manager for him. As I stood up, I felt his eyes on me and I continued to walk to the back and went to my manager's office.

"Hey Ms. Tosha, some guy is out here acting a fool about his order not being taken, and I'm on break," I said to her.

"I'm sorry boo, where the hell is Ebony?" she asked me. I shrugged my shoulders. "It's okay. I'll handle it. Go ahead and finish your break, you deserve that much," she told me. I went back to the front and smiled as she was walking behind me and said, "I apologize about the wait sir. Ms. Tosha will further assist you from here." He nodded his head as I walked from the back to go back to my table to finish my meal. He was something cute but I could do without the asshole qualities.

Jay

After the manager took my order, I decided to calm down some. I knew it wasn't ole girl fault but the shorty that was outside fussing with her dude said somebody would take our order after dude snatched her up from trying to come inside. As me and my homey was talking and waiting for our food, I kept stealing glances at the girl that I rolled up on about my food. I knew I should say something but when a nigga get hungry it's something else. She was beautiful though. She didn't have on any makeup, I could tell she was thick under that uniform and she was nice-nasty when she called herself checking me.

I had to chuckle at the thought cause that alone let me know she wasn't no pushover and the fact that she kept it cute when she came back out showed me just how mature lil mama was. I walked up to her after we were handed our food and stared until she noticed me.

"Can I help you sir? If there's anything wrong with your food just talk to the manager. I'm sure she'll fix it," She said.

"Everything good lil mama. My bad about earlier; a nigga like to eat and gets mad agitated when I'm hungry," I told her.

She nodded her head and said, "It's cool. Well, you fellas have a good night." She basically dismissed us with that one. I licked my lips and got turned on at the fact that she did that. I grabbed her phone from her and she gave me this death stare. I saw that she was listening to music and it was old school so I was with it. I went to her contacts and only saw four numbers in her phone. Why that's all she had I don't know but ain't been no niggas so I was good. I typed in my number and saved it in her phone and handed her the phone back to her and told her to call me. She rolled her eyes and said have a good night before putting her tray up and walking around the lobby cleaning up and checking on the other customers in there. I liked how she was. She was taking her job seriously and she had respect. I definitely was gonna see shorty again and make her mine.

It was a little after one a.m. and I had just dropped my homeboy off and was headed home for the night when I saw someone walking. Seeing as though my moms had gone through the same shit with me and my bro at a young age until she could afford to get a car, I felt the need to help whoever that was out. I busted a U-turn in the middle of the street and slowed down to whoever it was. When I lowered the window, I noticed it was shorty from the Burger King earlier.

"COOOH--COOOOH!" I called out to her as she kept walking. Either she didn't hear me or she was ignoring me. I called out to her again and she kept her head going forward. I sped up to a corner a few feet away, parked my car and got out, and jogged in her direction.

"Aye, lil mama, you need a ride," I said to her once I got up on her. She looked up at me, rolled her eyes and took out her headphones. "Aye, I saw you walking and was asking if you need a ride," I told her.

"Naw, I'm good, but thanks anyway," she said as she attempted to put her headphones back on.

I grabbed it and kept walking with her, "I gave you my number earlier why you ain't use it? I could've came and picked you up if you needed a ride," I said to her.

"I deleted it, plus I don't take rides from strangers," she said in a serious tone. I see she was gonna be a tough shell to crack.

"Well, I'm Jay, and it's nice to meet you. I don't like seeing people walk and I have a whole vehicle you can catch a ride in," I told her.

She just looked at me and said, "Well, Jay give someone else a ride."

I just laughed again because she was making me work. "Fuck it. I'll walk with you," I told her.

She stopped in her tracks and said, "Yeah right," I told her I was gonna walk with her so I was going to do it. I texted my homeboy to come scoop my car and told him I'd let him know where I ended up so that they could scoop me up.

"So tell me about yourself," I told her.

She laughed and kept walking so I decided to tell her about me. "Since you don't wanna talk, I will. My name is Jamal but I go by Jay. I am 18, I'm from Philly and just moved here about two weeks ago. I'm the youngest of me and my brother and I like making money and making my mama happy," I told her.

She smiled at how I just opened up to her. "Okay, I'm Roneshia, but everybody calls me RiRi. I'm 16, will be a senior next school year, and as you see, I work at Burger King," she said simply.

"No brothers or sisters," I pried.

"No, just me and my mama," she said.

I nodded my head understandingly. I then started asking her questions about what she wanted to do with her future and she gave me a little info about wanting to just make sure her mother was taken care of. I respected that because that is exactly how I was with my mama as well. We continued to walk for about three more miles before we turned onto a street that wasn't far from where my aunt lived. I sent my homeboy my location so that he could pull up with my car. I then walked her to her front door.

"So you gonna walk back to your car," she asked with a smile. She had such a beautiful smile that I almost got stuck in it.

"Hell no, my homeboy gonna be pulling up with my car. Before, I was walking with a purpose, but if I walked back, it wouldn't be with a purpose," I told her as she laughed. My homeboy pulled up and I nodded my head so that he'd know I'd be there in a second. "Well, let me hold yo phone again," I told her.

She rolled her eyes and handed me the phone as I placed my number back in it and this time I called my phone.

"Now why'd you do that," she said.

I smiled and said, "So that in case you delete my number again, I can still get in touch with you." She smiled and said goodnight before walking in the house. I made sure she locked the door before I went to the car. She just didn't know it yet, but she was gonna be my girl before the end of the summer.

RiRi

I had just snuck up to my room and was calling my mother to let her know I was home since I didn't see her car out front and was just about to close the door so that I could get some rest when my door swung back on me and knocked me in the face making me drop my phone.

"Daddy!!!!" I screamed.

"Don't daddy me you little bitch. Why the fuck when I got home you weren't here after school? You go to school and come home. And then you have the nerve to come back home after one in the morning and have some piss-tailed boy come with you!!!" he yelled as he threw a punch to my face like I was a man instead of his daughter.

I screamed out in pain as I felt blood gush from my nose and instantly felt the swelling. I screamed out again.

"Daddy, I have a job. I just got off of work and I didn't have any money to catch a cab. He saw me walking and--," I started as he swung on me again.

I started to try to run as I held my leaking face while trembling and trying not to cry. As he got closer to me, I instantly smelled the alcohol. He was drunk again and because my mama wasn't home he was taking it out on me.

"I don't give a fuck about you walking and him seeing you. You was supposed to have yo ass in this house when you got out of school," he roared as he took his belt off and commenced to whip me with it as if I was a child. Only difference was he was hitting me everywhere he could with it. I kept screaming and trying to get him off of me just as my mother came rushing in. I didn't even hear her come in.

"Lance, what the fuck are you doing, get off her!!" she yelled as she tried to tackle him. He immediately shook her off him as if he was trying to make a touchdown. He again swung the belt at me and this time it split my skin open on my arm as I screamed because of the open wound and agonizing pain. My mama grabbed a lamp out of the hallway and smashed it against his head. He stopped beating me and turned to her and swung his fist into her face and she flew into the wall. As soon as she hit the wall, he rushed her and started to choke her.

"Bitch, you taking this little whore's side. I'm your fuckin man, and you need to be helping me to whip that little bitch into shape instead of hitting me!" he yelled as he continued to choke her.

"L-L-Lance, sh-sh-she's our daughter," my mother stammered out.

"I don't give a fuck," he yelled as he continued to choke her. I tried to get up but was too weak and in too much pain but I had to do something. I finally was able to get up and grabbed the bat that was behind my room door and when he noticed me trying to hit him with it he dropped my mother and punched me in the face once again just as I heard a loud boom. I then heard feet running up the stairs as everything went black.

I woke up to sounds of beeping over and over. I tried to open my eyes to see what it was and where I was but it hurt to do so and one of my eyes had something over it. I immediately started panicking and was able to get the one that wasn't covered open. It was then I noticed a tube in my mouth and tubes in my nose. I was still trying to move and I heard another beeping noise speeding up and what sounded like an alarm. I then saw the outline of people rushing in but I couldn't quite see who they were.

I immediately got scared until someone touched me and said, "It's okay, Roneshia, we're gonna make sure you're okay. Let us just get these tubes out and we already called your mother so that she could come back in here. She stepped out to get something to eat so that's why you didn't see her when you woke up."

I nodded my head in understanding as a tear slid down my face. It stung while it rolled down and I kept trying to figure out where I was and why was I covered up like this.

"Okay, Roneshia, we need you to try to take a deep breath so we can remove the tube from your mouth and then we will give you some water so that you can talk a little okay," I heard a man's voice say.

I nodded my head once again and then I heard my mother's voice, "Oh, my God, RiRi, I am so sorry. I'm so sorry. I won't let anyone hurt you ever again. I'm so glad you woke up, baby, forgive me," she kept crying.

"Ms. Hart, please calm down so that she doesn't get worked up again. We need to keep her stabilized so that we can remove these tubes," I heard someone else say to her. She sniffled and mumbled okay. I was wondering what she was crying for and what this was all about and, just as the person removed the tube from my mouth and what felt like a bandage from my head, it suddenly hit me. I started to remember what happened when I got off work and my father attacked me and I tried to save my mother and I tried to scream and fight off whoever was touching me and they tried to hold me down as I started to cry and fight harder.

"We've gotta keep her stabilized!!! Mom, you need to go out in the hall so that we can calm her down before she sends herself into shock!!" the man's voice yelled.

I didn't want my mother to leave but my mouth was too dry to say anything as I tried to yell for her to not leave me. I then felt something stick me in my arm and suddenly I felt all the pain go away and felt like I was floating on air as my one eye got heavy. I started to drift back to sleep and slowly stopped trying to fight.

Tanya

The doctors finally let me back in RiRi's room and she was sleeping peacefully. I started to cry once again because I felt like I had failed my child. All I was trying to do was work more to get us out of the situation we were in. I couldn't just uproot her without a plan, so I just stayed and tried to figure it out the best way I could, by saving money to move somewhere else. I was so thankful when the young boy Jay and his friends busted in my house. When I called her phone and she didn't answer, I immediately started to panic, so I left work so that I could get home to her.

While driving there, I called again and she must not have known she picked up because all I could hear was her screaming so I broke every traffic law possible to get to my baby. Once there, I tried to fight Lance off of her and he tried to kill me for stopping him from trying to kill our daughter. He recently lost a position he wanted to someone else at work and slowly became an alcoholic.

At first, it wasn't so bad, until he started becoming aggressive with his alcohol. He then started slapping me around here and there and a few times raped me. When I threatened to leave, he'd throw it up in my face that I had nowhere to go, no money and then threatened to take my daughter's innocence from her. I stayed so that I could save enough money to make sure my daughter didn't have to want for anything and even let her start working to avoid him.

When he started to beat her, I knew then I needed to hurry up and get out of there. The fucked up part about it all is, he still has his job and can go to work like nothing ever happened and be normal for a while, but I had already fell out of love with him for the abuse he had done to me and was trying to do to my daughter.

I looked up when I felt someone walk into the room. "Hey, Ms. Tasha, how is she today?" Jay asked.

I looked at him and smiled as he walked closer with some flowers and a card. He had been here and doing this same thing for the last two days. She was knocked out into a coma so when she woke up it was a blessing.

"She woke up today and must've heard my voice while they were taking out the tubes and she started panicking and fighting so they sedated her and put her back to sleep, so she should be much calmer when she wakes back up but my baby is alive, so that's all that matters," I told him while crying.

He walked over to me and hugged me as I cried. While hugging him, I noticed a woman at the door with tears in her eyes and she asked if she could come in.

"Hi, I'm Jamal's mother, Crystal, and he filled me in on what was going on. I just came here to make sure everything was okay with your daughter, but from what I just heard, God is an on-time God and has already woken your sleeping beauty up for you," she said with a weak smile.

I nodded my head and stood up. "I'm Tasha, RiRi's mother, and thank you so much for raising such a fine young man and, Jamal, thank you once again for everything," I said as I hugged them.

When he and his friends came into my home they immediately pulled Lance away and started whooping his ass. Apparently, he had met my daughter at work that night and when she got off he noticed her walking. I was supposed to have the night off and got called in and texted her to let me know if she needed a ride home and I'd leave work to come and get her. He said that he offered her a ride and she refused so he got out and walked her home.

I felt like that was very nice of him. He waited until he heard the door lock before going back to his car and went around the corner to his aunt's house and drove back around to see if she'd like to get something to eat and saw the door cracked open and heard the tussling and screaming so he and his friends that were already with him busted in and saved us. I felt that I owed him my life for saving me and my daughter. He offered to kill Lance, but at this time, death was too good for him; he was gonna feel my pain.

I knew Jay must've thought I was gonna let this ride but that ain't even my M-O. I was gonna handle this in my own way. Since that night, Lance has been trying to come up here, but I wouldn't allow it. The way I saw it, he almost took me and my daughter out and I wouldn't allow him to try again. I heard RiRi stirring in the bed behind me and turned to look at her while she was waking up again.

I walked to the bed and grabbed her hands, "Sssh, baby, mommy's right here. I am so sorry he did this to you," I told her.

When she opened her eye fully she looked at me with tears. They were still bloodshot and the other was still bandaged. They said that with the force behind his punches, he popped a blood vessel in that eye and she could've possibly gone blind. I pray that she doesn't but whatever happens the fact that she's still alive is all that matters. I grabbed the cup of water the doctors and nurses left in the room for her and gave it to her with a straw.

After drinking a little she decided to speak to me, " Mommy, please tell me we're not going back. I don't wanna go back there again," she said.

I nodded my head and told her it was all gonna be okay and we didn't have to go back. I had already made up my mind to go into a hotel until either I saved enough money or my section 8 was approved. I wasn't too proud to get government assistance, especially in my time of need.

"We're not going back and I already talked to your manager and you still have your job, and your friend Jay is here. He's been here every day to make sure you're okay and even his mother is here now," I told her.

"What do you mean every day? How long was I out of it?" she asked.

"Two days," I told her. "Well, thank God I'm here and so are you," she said after taking a deep breath.

Jay then spoke up so that she'd know he was there, "Hey sleepy head," he said as her head snapped in the direction of his voice.

"What are you doing here," she said.

He chuckled and said, "Is that the thanks I get for saving your life." She just shook her head and chuckled to herself. While they were talking amongst themselves, his mother motioned for me to walk out in the hall to speak with her.

"I don't wanna overstep my boundaries, but I would like to help you guys if you allow me to. I've been in this kind of situation before when my oldest boy was around two years old, and I didn't really have anyone to help me out of it, so because I know how it feels to go through something like that, I'd like to offer you guys a place to stay in my home, so that you can save enough money to go wherever you're trying to move to. I have more than enough room since my sons decided to buy me a huge house they're barely in," she said.

"Thank you and I wouldn't want to impose. Do you think I can have some time to think about it and speak with my daughter because I don't want us to be in an uncomfortable situation," I told her.

She nodded her head understanding where I was coming from, "Well, I'd still like to exchange numbers to keep in contact with you guys, and if you need anything, I mean anything, don't hesitate to give me a call," she said.

We exchanged numbers and I gave her a hug because I appreciated everything she and her son had done for me and my daughter thus far, and it wasn't going unnoticed.

Jay

Seeing shorty banged up like that really fucked with me. I didn't believe in beating on women and/or your child for that matter. When I went back through to see if she wanted to go out with me to eat and noticed the door cracked, I knew something wasn't right. Then, I heard the screams and rumbling so I got out and motioned for my niggas that was in the car behind mine to come with me.

When I saw him knock shorty out and try to go back to her moms I lost it. I tried to beat him to death but Ms. Tasha wouldn't let me but she said she'd handle it. If she take too long I was gonna make his ass feel me. I been coming back to the hospital every day to see her in between me working these streets. It had been two weeks since the incident and she was finally being released today. She told me about her only being able to see shadowy outlines out of her eye, but over the days she finally was able to see again. They unwrapped her other eye and we thought she'd be blind in it but besides the red in it from where the blood vessel popped she was able to see out of it perfectly. He had fractured her nose as well, but I was able to get the doctor to fix that for her, too. She was definitely gonna be my girl, and I was gonna make sure no harm came to her ever again.

With me coming to the hospital to see her, we got to know each other a little more and I was glad. It just sucked that it was on these terms. I was glad when her mother agreed to staying with my moms temporarily. Since my aunt was a real estate agent, we were working on surprising them with a new house so that they wouldn't have to stay with us too long and be uncomfortable. I was gonna pick her up from the hospital but her moms wanted to do it herself and spend alone time with her and I respected that.

While she was doing that, I decided to relieve some stress and slide up on my homegirl Tisha. Tisha was this chick that stayed on Eastside that I met when we first moved down south that was cool to hold shit for me, and she put me up on game on the who's who so I wouldn't step on any toes while putting my name in the streets. She was also a baddie that I would fuck with from time to time just to get a quick nut in. Instead of calling her, I just went over to her house and turned the doorknob to her front door to go inside. When it didn't open, and I noticed it was locked, I then knocked. She was the type of bitch to leave the door unlocked for a nigga to come thru to get straight and only kept it locked if she was entertaining someone. She opened the door and looked at me smiling. When she let me in, there was a nigga sitting on her couch chilling so I nodded my head what's up in his direction before he got up and left. I felt like I knew him from somewhere, but hell, it could be from here.

She locked the door and made sure her back door was locked as well and led me to the bedroom where she got on her knees to unbuckle my pants. I put my hands on her and said, "Nah ma, you know the drill. That pussy need to be cleaned first."

"I took a shower earlier today," she whined.

"Shit, and you probably been running around since then and not only that another nigga just been in here. He could've smashed before I got here. So the pussy needs to be squeaky clean before I get in there," I told her. She stood up pouting like a big ass kid and then walked into the bathroom to shower. I sat on her bed while she did that and rolled up. I also kept checking her blinds to make sure her neighborhood was the same that it was when I rolled up minus the car that was there when I got there to ensure shawty wasn't setting me up. She walked out of the bathroom about ten minutes later smelling like that pear scented Bath and Body Works.

I smiled and said, "That's better." She told me to shut up and stuck her tongue out at me as I told her to put that mouth to use. She smiled and got down on her knees and took my nine inches into her mouth. She began to suck the soul out of my shit and instead of me moaning like I wanted to do, I just grabbed the back of her head and fucked her mouth crazy while she sat there moaning and playing with herself.

After I busted in her mouth, she started to suck me off again to get me back up and, when she did, she turned around and tried to sit on my dick and I almost punched the fuck out of her.

"YOO, slow down, I ain't even got my rubber on yet," I told her.

"My bad, you know I wanna feel you so bad you can go in naked if you want," she said with lust-filled eyes.

"Nah, I'll pass. I ain't tryna have no kids witcha and you cool and all but you know you a passaround," I told her.

She looked at me as if she was hurt and wanted to cry but quickly shook it off. I grabbed my own rubber out of my pocket and slid it on cause I was serious about what I said about her being a passaround, and I ain't tryna catch shit. Once I got the condom on comfortably, I let her slide down on my shit to ride. For a hoe, she was tighter than most hoes I dealt with but not too tight. She squeezed her muscles as she rode and, at first, I was into it then I started to feel guilty as if I was cheating on RiRi. I started to pump faster as if I was gonna nut just to hurry her along as she screamed like her life depended on it and my dick got softer.

When she finally came, she dropped on my chest, and I gently pushed her off, took the empty condom off and went to the bathroom to flush it. At first, I was gonna stay and smoke and chill with her but I'd rather check up on my future so I left some bills on the dresser for Tisha as she lightly snored and took a quick birdbath in the bathroom before heading out. I made sure to put the bottom lock on her front door on my way out.

On my way to my mama's crib, I stopped at the store to grab some balloons and three dozen roses, one dozen for my mama, a dozen for Ms. Tasha, and a dozen for RiRi. I also grabbed some Chinese food for RiRi since she was talking about it the whole time she was in the hospital and I texted my moms to let her and Ms. Tanya know they didn't have to cook tonight. I got enough food for everyone and made my way to the house.

On the way, I started to get calls on my business phone about my niggas needing a reup at one of the trap houses I had. I told them the shipment wouldn't be in until tomorrow, so they could shut down for the night. I pulled up to the house that my brother and I purchased for our mother and smiled at how far we'd all come and the fact that I could spend that money on my mother. I grabbed all the food out of the car just as my brother Justin pulled up with his on-again, off-again girlfriend Zee, and he grabbed the food as I said what's up to Zee while I grabbed the roses out of the car. We walked into the house where my mama, Ms. Tasha, and RiRi were all sitting talking and laughing.

"Hey y'all, I stopped and got some Chinese food since somebody been talking about it the whole time they were in the hospital," I said as they all laughed. I then walked up to each of them and gave them their roses and a peck on the cheek.

"Aww, thank you son, that was sweet of you," my mother said as Ms. Tasha and RiRi thanked me as well.

"Where's mine since you wanna be buying roses for everybody," Zee said.

My mother rolled her eyes and said, "I know you ain't in my house and didn't speak."

"Sorry, Ms. Crystal. How y'all doing? I'm Zee, Justin's girlfriend," she said all phony like.

"UHH, friend, cause we ain't back together right now," Justin told her as me and my mother laughed and RiRi and her mother shrugged their shoulders at us. She frowned at him and looked slightly embarrassed.

"I'm Justin, Jay's older brother and mama's finest son," he said laughing as I playfully swung at him.

"Nice to meet you. Crystal, you raised some very charming young men," Ms. Tasha said.

"Thank you girl," she said as they walked into the kitchen to put the roses in vases and to get the food together that I bought.

"How you feeling little bit. My brother and mama told me about you and I'm glad to see you're feeling better and you and yo moms gonna be staying here for a little bit," Justin said.

"Uh, what do you mean she'll be staying here," Zee said with attitude.

"UH, just like I said. This my mama house and she can have whoever she wants in her shit. You don't even pay yo own bills so don't question what's going on where I pay bills at," he said shutting her up.

She looked him up and down like she had a problem and then I knew she would make it a problem since she was friends with Tisha.

She turned to me and said, "So, Jay, how's Tisha doing?"

I laughed and said, "She good. She fell asleep when I was over her house not too long ago. Why don't you call her if you wanna know how she doing." She smirked like that was what she wanted to do anyway. "How are you feeling RiRi?" I asked her as she smiled.

"I'm feeling better now that I'm out of that damn hospital. And thanks for everything and I really mean it; you're a great friend. I'm glad that you were persistent when we met," she said.

I smiled back but my smile wouldn't reach all the way up to my eyes. I'm not sure why the words *"you're a great friend*" bothered me so much but it did.   Zee and Justin argued a little back and forth and he ended up calling her a cab to take her back home and we headed into the kitchen with my mother and Ms. Tasha with dinner while RiRi dozed off from the pain medicine she was prescribed. After we finished eating and cleaned up the kitchen, I put her food up for when she woke up ready to eat and I laid down on the couch facing where she was laying sleeping and watched her sleep until sleep came over me as well.

RiRi

I jumped up out of my sleep sweating and looking around. For a minute, I couldn't remember where I was. When I looked over and saw a body on the couch facing the one I was laying across from, and noticed that it was Jay, I remembered where I was and immediately started to feel better. I laid back down since I was still in a lot of pain from what my father did to me. I was still having nightmares about that night and each time it seemed to get worse. For example, the dream I just had, he was successful in killing my mother and almost killed me as well but I woke up before he could.

It all felt so real. I was just glad when my mother agreed to come stay here so that I didn't have to worry about him trying to track us down if we had went to a hotel. I couldn't really go back to sleep because the dream had me so shook so I decided to just get up and see if there was any food left from earlier since Ms. Crystal had already told me I could make myself at home. I took my time and stood up from the couch since I was still in some pain from the bruising on my ribs. I still don't understand how I made it out with only bruising, a broken nose, and my eye messed up. The way he was whooping on me I'd think I'd come out with more damage or without my life.

As I started towards the kitchen, I thought I heard footsteps behind me, but since it was dark I couldn't make out anything. I decided to just speed up to the kitchen so that I could turn the lights on to make sure I could see everything. As I started walking faster, I heard the footsteps walking faster behind me. Just as I reached the kitchen and tried to find the light switch someone grabbed me, and I screamed at the top of my lungs trying to swing on the person at the same time.

"Yo, Ri baby, calm down, it's just me. It's okay," Jay said as he tried to restrain me and calm me down just as lights came on in the house and my mother, his mother and brother rushed into the area to see what was going on.

"Jamal, what the fuck are you doing to the girl," she yelled rushing to my side along with my mother as I tried to stop crying and catch my breath.

"Nothing, ma, she woke up and I noticed her struggling to get to the kitchen so I got up to help her," he said just as his mother punched him in the chest.

"Breathe, baby; is that all that happened," my mother said a little apprehensive. I had to fix it and quick because his mother didn't have to take us in, but she did and I didn't want to ruin anything. I finally was able to talk.

"I, I, I woke up because of a nightmare. I tried to go back to sleep and couldn't, s-s-so I got up to see if there was anything left to eat, and while I was walking towards the kitchen, I heard footsteps behind me. The faster I moved, the faster the footsteps were and, when I reached the kitchen, he gave me a light tap on the arm and it scared me.

I thought dad had found us," I said trying not to cry again. I felt it was better to say tap instead of grab so that they wouldn't misinterpret what I was meaning.

"Sssh, baby, it's okay. How long have you been having nightmares?" my mother said as she held me in her arms.

"Since I woke up," I told her.

"Why didn't you tell me," she said pulling back to look at me.

"I didn't want to upset or worry you. You already blame yourself for what happened and it's neither of our faults," I told her.

She looked at me with tears in her eyes and nodded. "Ri, I'm sorry. I didn't mean to scare you. I just wanted to make sure you wasn't sleep walking and wanted to make sure you were okay," he said.

I nodded my head and motioned for him to come here so that we could hug it out. We did and everyone decided that they wanted to stay up. We all went in the kitchen and Jay heated up the food he fixed for me earlier and I ate it all happy that I could finally have my Chinese food. They decided to get a game of spades going as my mother and Ms. Crystal decided to be on teams against Jay and Justin who were on team. I started to get sleepy again but I didn't want to ruin the night so I told them I'd be right back and sat on the couch just to fall asleep again.

Not long after, I felt myself being lifted off the couch and looked to see if I was floating and noticed I was in Jay's arms. He looked at me looking at him and whispered, "I got you, ma. I always got you. Nobody gonna hurt you ever again." I nodded my head and laid back on his chest and went back to sleep. For some odd reason, I believed him.

The next morning, I woke up in a bedroom that was set up with some of the same things that I had in my bedroom at home, only the room was bigger, and I had a futon in the room as well. I noticed the bedroom door was shut and that there was a blanket thrown across the futon as if someone had been in there asleep with me. I hoped like hell it was Jay and that my nightmares weren't coming to life. I sat up and saw there was an adjoining bathroom to the bedroom so I went in there to use it and decided to take a shower and brush my teeth. It was a bit of a struggle, but I wasn't gonna let any pain stop me from washing my body. Hygiene is very important to me.

I closed my eyes as I let the hot water run over my body. I thought I heard someone call my name over the water, but I was too focused on how good this shower water was feeling at the moment. I just held my head under the water and let it take me to a faraway place in my mind. I suddenly felt a cold draft of air and looked towards the door and saw Jay standing there with a breakfast tray in his hands just looking at me. Instead of covering up and getting shy, I grabbed the body wash in the bathroom and washed my body while making eye contact with him. I didn't do anything in a provocative way, but I just wanted him to know that I saw him watching me while I watched him watch me. I wasn't really that shy about my body or anything. I knew what I had on me and that I was one of the few black girls that was naturally thick, but I couldn't hide it even if I tried. I just took care of myself with the shape that I had.

"My bad," he said as he backed out of the bathroom and went back into the room. I just shrugged my shoulder and continued to wash. When I finished, I got out of the shower, dried off, brushed my teeth, and headed into the bedroom where there was a pair of pink sweatpants and slippers along with a t-shirt for me to put on. After getting dressed, I noticed the food tray that Jay had was on the nightstand with some scrambled eggs with cheese, cheese grits, corned beef hash, crispy bacon, and some orange juice and fruit on the side. I knew my mother had something to do with the breakfast meal because those were all my favorite breakfast items.

There was a knock at the door and it was Ms. Crystal, "Good morning, baby, how you feeling?" she asked.

"I feel a little better. Just wish this pain would go away so that I can go back to work," I told her.

"Trust me, I understand. I apologize about last night when Jamal scared you; he didn't mean any harm. He even slept in here last night and brought a night light in here so you'd notice him if you woke up," she said as I chuckled about the night light.

"It's okay. I know he didn't mean any harm. The dream I had just had me really shook so I got scared thinking he had found us," I said.

She nodded her head and said, "Okay, just wanted to make sure you were okay. Oh, and your mother stepped out for a bit and said that she'd be back but to text or call her if you needed anything." I nodded and said okay as she stood up and left the room.

I sat on the bed and began to eat just as there was another knock on the door. I said come in thinking it must've been Ms. Crystal coming back to the room, but it was Jay.

"What's up," I said.

"Uhh nothing much. My bad about earlier. Matter fact, what was up with that in the bathroom earlier?" he said.

"Um, I was taking a shower. You came in for whatever reason, which I assume was because of breakfast and I was washing and continued to wash my body, and not in a sexual way, just me washing," I said matter of factly.

"So you don't think you was being sexual with the way you was looking me in the eyes," he tried to argue.

"No I don't. I think I like to look people in the eyes and you decided to come into the bathroom while I was showering and I wanted to finish my shower. Nothing more, nothing less," I said.

He huffed and nodded his head as if he finally understood. He decided to turn on the TV that I didn't even know was in there and put on a movie. We decided on *Girls Trip* since it had now become one of my favorite movies to watch. I was dozing off when Jay's phone kept going off. He got up and checked to see if I was still asleep, kissed me on the cheek and said he'll be back. When he left out of the room, I drifted off to sleep just to end up dreaming about what could've happened when he came in the bathroom.

Tisha

I was a little pissed about the way that Jay had done me. He knew I was gonna be down for him if he let me.

Yeah, a bitch had a little whore in her, but damn that don't mean I can't tone it down. Then, my bitch Zee calls me going off on how Justin sent her home in a cab because she was mad that Jay was at their mother's house and had some little bitch living there in the house with him, his mama, and brother and had the nerve to bring her and her mama roses along with his mama. Why he got her there, I don't know. I mean, what the fuck can she do for him that I can't? I got my own place and car, this bitch living with his mama and brought her mama in the mix. What kind of bitch can't handle her own? The shit just pisses me off.

I decided to hit him up and confront him about it all, because I was tired of being all these niggas' fantasies instead of their reality to come home to. Jay already had a name for himself and was making it bigger and I wanted to be right there when he got all the way to the top. I was hornier than a mothafucka, but I couldn't bring none of my hoes over here since one was here yesterday when Jay came by. He was right. I had fucked that nigga, but shit, my pussy stayed leaking like a pipe that's about to burst. If he fucked me regularly like I was his bitch, he wouldn't have this problem.

My doorbell rang, and I knew it was Jay because I had my door locked so no one would be tempted to walk in. They knew if the door was unlocked come on in and get right to it. But if it was locked, I was entertaining. I did good for myself as a hoe. I ain't never had no STDs, kept my shit tight, and no abortions. I walked to the door and opened it up for *my* man and let him in.

"What's up baby," I said to him and tried to take his clothes off.

He pushed my hands away and said, "Man, I ain't feeling this shit Tisha. We can still be cool on the friend tip, but I ain't tryna fuck with you no more like that." When he said that, I felt like I was gut punched.

"What do you mean. We do more than just that and we both got needs," I said to him while silently getting pissed.

"Man, Tisha, I ain't even tryna go there withchu right now. I don't feel like this shit is going anywhere withchu," he said as he tried to walk away from me.

"What do you mean? I can help make it go somewhere, just let me. Just give me an opportunity to show you." I tried again to unbuckle his pants and he shoved me hard and I hit the floor. I slowly looked up at him with fake tears in my eyes, "It's because of her isn't it?" I asked.

"What, man you don't even know whatchu talkin about." He said as he dismissed me.

"Oh, I know. Zee told me all about the little young bitch at yo house witcho mama and her mama. What I gotta give up, my independence for you to want me rather than some young bitch!!" He moved so fast I couldn't even blink.

He yoked me up and had his hand around my throat and squeezed a little before speaking.

"Watch your mothafuckin mouth bitch! You don't even know her so don't let no typa foul shit about her come out of yo mouth again. Yeah, you and me had a little fun here and there, but bitch, I can't wife yo hoe ass!! She may be young and got her mama with her, but hell they going through some shit and, not only that, she got something that you don't. She got drive and goals. You just out for a nut and some money, but bitch yo mouth may be good at what it do but it won't make a nigga like me wife you!"

With that, he let me go as I gasped for air and dropped to the floor with tears in my eyes. He looked at me, shook his head and walked away. I was more pissed than hurt. I wasn't in love with him, but I was in love with what he could do. That's why I tried so hard to make him fall in love with me. It usually was never this hard. I felt like I had to pull out the big guns now. I picked up my cell phone and called a number.

The person on the other line picked up and said, "What's good, you finally came to yo senses with what we talked about?"

I cleared my throat before speaking, "Yeah, I just don't want him hurt because I have more unfinished business with him that needs to get handled."

The person on the other line laughed and said, "Bitch, you gotta do more than that. I need real info right about now. But anyway, I'll see what I can do. I'm bout to slide up on you in a few though aight?" he said.

I nodded my head as if he could see me and said okay. I hung up the phone wondering if what I was going to do was worth it but just as quickly as the thought entered my mind it left as well. It damn sure was worth it.

Jay

I thought about me cutting Tisha off and knew it was the best decision for me to do. If I wanted a future with RiRi, especially after everything she's been through, I needed to cut off anything toxic. Tisha was cool, but the bitch was toxic. She wanted more than I was willing to give her. All I was willing to give her was a nut here and there and that's it. This bitch wanted to be wifey, but you couldn't be wifey while fucking me and everybody else in the hood.

After leaving her place, I headed back to my moms' house to see if I could get RiRi to get out of the house for a little bit. I didn't want her to feel as if she had to be confined to the house all the time. As I drove down the highway towards my mom's house, I felt like something wasn't right. I started to check my surroundings and noticed a car following me. For some reason, the car looked oddly familiar, but I just couldn't place where I had seen it before. I started to make some turns and remained at a steady speed and noticed the car still following me. I picked up my phone and dialed up my brother so that I could tell him what was going on.

"Sup," he said into the phone with music blaring.

"Ayo, bruh, I think somebody following me," I said into the phone as I hit the gas to speed up. The car behind me sped up as well.

I could hear the music being lowered in the background as he spoke back into the phone, "Where you coming from?"

"Shit, just left Tisha's house to break things off with her and was headed towards moms and noticed the car behind me. I tried to shake them to see if it was a coincidence but I don't think it is," I told him.

He sighed and said, "Where you at now." I looked up at some signs and saw Morrison Ave. I told him where and he said, "Okay, I'm gonna try and get out there, just try to lose whoever it is and I'm coming."

Just as I was about to answer him, the car slammed into the back of my car and I dropped my phone while yelling, "Oh, shit!" I heard Justin yell my name in the phone while it was laying on the floor of the car. I sped up and reached under my seat and grabbed my gun as the car tried to hit me again and I swerved out of the way. I sped up some more and noticed another car headed in my direction with the windows down and someone aiming a gun out of their window at me, "FUCK!!!" I yelled as I tried to maneuver my car out of their window.

I aimed my gun back at the car with one hand as I steered with the other hand. Suddenly, before I could pull the trigger, bullets started to head my way, "Shit," I said while trying to get the car out of the way of bullets and the other car trying to take me off the road. I ducked as the bullets began to riddle my car and burst through my windows. I kept trying to figure a way to get myself out of this predicament. Suddenly, I saw myself getting closer to the interstate. I wanted to avoid getting myself fucked up more while on a bridge.

I decided to just try my luck with slamming on breaks to get the other car off of me and to distract the shooters. I could hear sirens in the distance but the shooters weren't letting up. I made sure I had my seatbelt on tight and slammed on my breaks causing the other car that kept trying to ram me to swerve and flip over in the middle of the road while the shooters swerved to avoid hitting them. When I noticed that they were distracted with that and saw smoke in the air, I hopped out of my car and ran in the opposite direction as fast as I could. I slowed down when I got about five miles away and got near a shopping center. I walked into the nearest store that I saw and asked to use the phone.

The young lady at the entrance handed me her phone and said, "Oh, my god, you're bleeding, are you okay." That was the last thing I heard after dialing my brother's number.

Tanya

I was so thankful for Crystal and her hospitality and knew once I got back on my feet the way that I wanted to I was definitely gonna look out. I hit up my best friend Gladys to come through so we could head out. I was just finishing up getting dressed when I heard the doorbell ring. I heard screams then laughter so I figured Crystal had met Gladys. I walked out of the bedroom that she gave me to live in and headed to the living room and saw them laughing and hugging.

"Bitch, you didn't tell me that the lady helping you out was my sister," Gladys said.

I looked puzzled and said, "Y'all are sisters."

They started to laugh and Crystal said, "Hell yeah, we got the same father but we grew up knowing one another. I was in Philly but would come visit or her mother would let her come up there to stay with us during vacations or just cause."

I smiled glad that they had known each other all along and that they both got along. "Sis, you rolling with us," Gladys asked Crystal.

I shook my head at Gladys because I wasn't sure if Crystal would want to be in that type of situation that we were about to insert ourselves into.

"Hell yeah, you know I'm always down to get out of this house," Crystal said.

"Well, Crystal, this ain't no ordinary ride out witcha girls day," I told her.

"Girl, boo, where you think my boys get they thug from," she said.

When she reached under a table near where she was standing and pulled out a gun all I could do was smile and respect her gangsta.

"Aight, well, I guess we out ladies. RiRi is asleep and Jay said he was gonna come back to try and take her out today after he finished handling some business," I said. They both nodded and said cool.

We headed outside while Crystal locked up the house and got into the hoopty that Gladys was driving to take us on this mission that we had set up. We headed to my old house and sat in the car until we saw another car pull up. The guys in the car looked at us and nodded towards the house and we nodded our heads. They got out of their car and walked up to the front door and rang the doorbell. When Lance answered the door, one guy just punched him in the head one time and he was knocked out. That was my nigga One Down because all it took was one hit and whoever he hit was down.

We drove off as One Down and the guy with him grabbed Lance up and walked him out to the car like they were all fucked up drunk and laughed like there was a joke being told. We headed towards the warehouse where I used to put in work at, and I shook my head thinking on how I had to go back to my old ways to handle this situation. I walked into the warehouse and headed to the back room where they'd be bringing Lance when they arrived. I walked around trying to think of what I'd like to use to torture him and, then I saw some tools left on the floor. I heard the door open and smiled as Crystal and Gladys stood on either side of me.

"Damn, y'all two back out here together? I know more than his shit about to get fucked up," One Down said as we all laughed.

He then sat Lance down in a chair in the middle of the room as his homeboy tied him up with some rope that he had in his hand when they came in. After they finished, Crystal took a bucket full of bleach that she found and splashed it on Lance as he jumped and woke up.

"Wh- what the fuck!! Bitch, you better untie me before I beat your ass and that little bitch you call my daughter!!" he yelled.

This nigga really had heart threatening me like he was and he was the one that was tied to a chair.

"On second thought, One Down untie this bitch. I wanna fuck him up with a fair fight," I said.

One Down looked at me for a second before Gladys nodded for him to just do it. He untied Lance while his homey held a gun to Lance's head so that he could ensure him not to do anything. Once they finished, Lance stood up and shook his head at me and said, "Bitch, I see you got some balls trying to come at me like you are. You got ten minutes after I'm done fucking you up to go get my daughter and bring y'all asses back home."

Laughing, I said, "Funny, I thought I was running the show and you think I'm gonna listen to you. You got me fucked up Lance."

He smirked and said, "I see me knocking you upside the head made you forget who the fuck I am." He walked towards me and One Down tried to grab him but I told him just let him come. When he got near me and tried to slap me, I sidestepped him and hit him with a right hook. After that, I swung at him again and started to throw jabs his way. He lost his footing and fell. When he fell, I started to walk away because I wasn't gonna hit someone while they were down, but when I did that he grabbed my leg and pulled me down with him and punched me in the face. When he did that, I lost it.

He tried to choke me while still punching at me and Gladys came and took the hammer that I found and swung it at his head. Crystal came next with a screwdriver and jabbed it in his arm as he screamed out in pain. I pushed him off me with blood coming down my face and picked up the power drill and drilled nails in his hand to the floor. He screamed and tried to move his hand from the floor. Crystal kicked him in the face and he tried to grab his face with the other hand and when he did that I drilled the other hand to his face as he screamed again.

When he did that, Crystal grabbed the hammer that was now near her and started to hammer the nail that was already in his hand on the floor more into his hand. He now had snot and tears running down his face.

"I-I-I'm sorry. P-P-P-Please stop!!" he screamed like a little bitch.

He had me fucked up if he thought I would've just let him off that easy. Gladys smiled and said, "You want us to get your hand from the floor." He nodded and that quick she took a machete that she had hidden from behind her back and chopped his hand off that was nailed to the floor. She then pulled the nail from his hand with the back of the hammer and threw it at him while he was still screaming. By this time, there was blood everywhere and he was losing consciousness. I was surprised he was still alive with the other hand nailed to his face.

"There you go," Gladys said with a crazy look on her face. Me and Crystal laughed and then I took the screwdriver that was still in his side and used it to push the nail further into his face as he collapsed and started to gurgle on his blood. He looked me in my eyes with fear on his face before his eyes started roll to the back of his head. I pulled the screwdriver from his face and jabbed it right into his Adam's apple to ensure he was dead.

"That was fun, we need to do this again," Crystal said while clapping her hands. We looked at each other and laughed at her being silly like a child. I nodded my head to One Down so that he could take care of cleanup and told the ladies to come on so we could get out of these messy clothes. There was a room in the warehouse with a shower in it so that we all could handle our hygiene and it also had clothes there just for instances like this. After I finished washing, Gladys went next and then Crystal. While Crystal was showering, her phone kept going off. Finally it stopped ringing and Glady's phone started to ring as Crystal was walking out the bathroom.

"Hey- where y'all at!! We on the way!!" Gladys shouted.

"What's wrong," Crystal said.

Gladys looked her in the eyes and said, "Jay got shot."

RiRi

I had just woken up and felt a sharp pain in my chest and didn't know where it was coming from. I got up and looked around the house and noticed I was there alone. I decided that I'd be useful and make something to eat for everyone for when they all got back. I went to the kitchen to see what all Ms. Crystal had up in there. I ended up finding some porkchops and potatoes and decided to go from there.

I washed the porkchops and some green onions and seasoned the porkchops. I then put some Italian dressing and Worcestershire sauce in the pan I'd be using to have the base ready and commenced to adding my other ingredients to the smothered porkchops I'd be making. I also made some mashed potatoes and gravy from scratch as our sides and made some snap green beans as well. I was getting hungrier while cooking everything.

When I was finished cooking, I sat down and said grace and began to slowly take my time to eat. I then put up individual plates for everyone and put up the leftovers in case anyone would want seconds. I noticed that it was going on eight o'clock and no one made it home yet. I picked up my phone and called Jay and his phone kept ringing. I had really begun to enjoy his company and the talks that we'd have and was missing him right now. I then called my mother to see where she was.

"Hello," she said out of breath.

"Ew, Ma, if you was doing something, why you answer the phone?" I said disgustedly.

"Oh hush, I'm running to the ER to make sure Crystal don't act too much of an ass," she said as my ears perked up.

"ER for what?" I asked her.

She paused for a second and took a deep breath and then spoke, "Jay got shot sweetie-,"

I didn't hear what else she said because I dropped my phone and immediately jumped up to head to the hospital. I was so busy getting myself ready that I didn't hear my mother yelling through the phone. I picked up the phone after I had finished getting myself together and said,

"Sorry about that ma. I kind of got upset but I just got dressed so I'm gonna have an uber bring me there. Which hospital are you guys at?" I asked while pulling up my uber app.

"We're at the hospital downtown on Meeting St. It's not too far from the house, but please be careful. Call or text me as soon as you get in the uber," she said.

I told her okay and headed outside just as my uber pulled up. I got in and told the young lady where I was going. I texted my mother informing her that I was in the uber and that I would be at the hospital shortly. When we made it to the hospital, I tipped my driver and headed in through the emergency entrance and was greeted with yelling and cussing.

"I DON'T GIVE A FUCK WHAT Y'ALL SAYING!! I'M NOT LEAVING THIS MOTHAFUCKIN HOSPITAL UNTIL SOMEBODY TELL ME WHAT THE FUCK IS GOING ON WITH MY MOTHAFUCKIN CHILD!!!!"

If this wasn't a serious moment, I would've laughed at Ms. Crystal going ham the way that she was. I walked up to her and gave her a hug and rubbed her back to ensure her that it would all be okay. She stopped her rant for a brief second and embraced me and cried on my shoulder. I just held her as my mother and her friend whom I called Aunt Gladys walked up and embraced us as well. I noticed Justin in the background with red eyes that I could tell he was crying from.

Once I was able to get out of their embrace, I hugged him to let him know it'd all be okay. Just as we were releasing our hug, I heard a voice yell, "I know the fuck you ain't got your homeless ass on my fucking man!! Bitch, you can't get Jay so now you want my nigga!"

When Zee got closer, I pretended that I was gonna walk away but I punched that bitch so hard you'd think someone had just hammered a nail in the wall with the way she flew and how loud that pop was.

"I done had enough of you disrespecting me bitch. I'm here to make sure my *friend,* a really good friend of mine, is okay. I am hugging his brother and mother ensuring they're okay mentally which is what the fuck you should be doing if you so-called here for your man. You betta get some act right, bitch, before I give it to you," I told her as security rushed in our direction.

I walked away and looked at her as she held her face and cried because Justin didn't help her up. She'll be alright, though. *She's here for all the wrong reasons*, I thought to myself. I walked back to my mother who winked at me and listened intently as she and Aunt Gladys told me what happened with Jay, from him being on the phone with his brother, to him getting shot at and borrowing someone's phone to call Justin and the person getting him to the hospital because he passed out from his loss of blood.

Just then, some chick burst in through the doors looking flustered and Zee rushed to her and pointed in the direction that I was in with my mother, Ms. Crystal and Aunt Gladys. When I noticed her with a scowl on her face as she headed in our direction, I immediately knew she would be a problem as well. She was cute but doing entirely too much coming to the hospital dressed like a hoochie mama.

She walked up to us and said, "Hi, I'm Tisha, Jay's girlfriend."

When she said that, I wanted to laugh because he had already told me how they were just friends with benefits but she wanted more and he didn't. He also told me how she and Zee were good friends and I thought it was pretty ironic that she rushed here dressed like that because I was here.

"My son don't got no girlfriend; he got a future wife and it ain't you hoe," Ms. Crystal said.

Tisha's eyes damn near popped out of her head at what Ms. Crystal said to her. I just smirked and looked on as the doctor came out and called out for us to tell us the status of Jay's condition.

"Hi, I'm Dr. Green, and I'm working on Mr. Jamal Miller this evening," he said as he extended his hand to Ms. Crystal to shake.

"Thank you, I'm his mother, and you've already met my other son and this is the rest of the family here. So how's he doing?" Ms. Crystal asked.

"Well, with the severity of what his injury should've been, I'm happy to say that he's up and about right now. He was shot near his rib but the bullet went in and out without hitting any major arteries. He's a pretty lucky young man because from what I see it should've done more damage but God is on his side. We gave him some pain meds but it doesn't seem as if he's in any pain at all. He's giving us a hard time wanting to leave but he's also asking if a RiRi is here. Other than that, he's doing fine."

We all let out a breath that we were holding unanimously. I stepped forward and said, "That's me, I'm here."

"Okay, then, if you and mom will follow me to his room, maybe you can help calm him and talk to him. We only want to keep him overnight to make sure there is nothing else going on," Dr. Green said.

We nodded as me and Ms. Crystal got ready to walk to Jay's room with Dr. Green. I looked over at the Tisha chick on her phone trying to be discreet, and that just didn't seem right to me. Something was up with this bitch, and I wanted to find out.

As we walked into his room, we could hear him loudly saying to the nurses, "Man, listen, I don't need to stay in this bitch. Clean this room up for somebody that needs to be in here. I got shit to do and keeping me in here ain't gonna do shit but piss me the fuck off."

Me and Ms. Crystal looked at each other and laughed as we walked further into his room so that he could see us.

"Damn, baby boy, don't take they heads off," Ms. Crystal said as she walked closer to him and gave him a hug.

I could see a look of satisfaction cross her face knowing that her son was okay.

"Ma, you know they can't hold a real one down," he said as we all laughed. He looked at me and it felt as if he was staring through my soul. "Come here RiRi," he said.

"I'll go back in the waiting area and let everyone know you're okay. I just wanted to lay eyes on you first to know in my heart my baby boy is fine," Ms. Crystal said.

I nodded as he said nothing and continued to stare at me. I walked to him as he sat up in the bed and the nurses and his mother exited the room and shut the door behind them. I kept eye contact with him as I got closer to his hospital bed. As soon as I reached the bed, he snatched me up in his arms and began kissing me deeply. I was caught off guard at first but then I continued to kiss him back. He pulled me on top of him in the bed and began to rub my body while kissing me. Suddenly, we heard the door open. I attempted to get up but Jay kept holding me closer as he continued to kiss me.

"Ahem," we heard a voice say as they cleared their throat.

I turned and saw Tisha standing there with a scowl on her face. I smiled and sat up as I let Jay see who had interrupted us.

"What the fuck do you want Tisha?" he asked.

She had a hurt look on her face and said, "Really Jay. You gone do me like that for some homeless bitch?"

I guess she didn't witness me rock her girl earlier in the lobby. I finally took the anger out on her that I had felt for my father and anyone else that wronged me. I walked up on her and punched her with a right hook. She tried to keep her footing and swing back but she was too slow. I swung again and this time I decided to use my other hand to connect to her face as I slammed her face against the wall in his room. I must've blacked out because next thing I knew I was being lifted in the air and when I looked down she was in a heap of blood on the floor. Jay had me in his arms as hospital security and the nurses filed in along with our mothers and Aunt Gladys.

"Damn, baby girl, you just kicking ass today hunh?" Aunt Gladys said.

If I weren't so pissed, I'd laugh. The doctor rushed in and looked from me and Jay to the floor at Tisha and some of the nurses were trying to clean her up and help regain her consciousness.

"You need to leave now!! Security please escort-" the doctor started as Jay cut him off.

"I'll take her but if y'all come over here and touch her it won't end well." He gave them all a death stare as they backed up.

"Mr. Miller, we need to keep you for observation to make sure-"

Jay held up his hand at the doctor and said, "My nigga, I don't wanna stay in this bitch. I gotta go and make sure my girl good and that's what I'm about to do. Y'all fix up the hoe as best as y'all can and just give me my pain meds and I'm out." The doctor just looked at him and nodded his head. Ms. Crystal, who I didn't know was standing there said she'll get everything told Justin to take me and Jay home. Jay put me down and gathered his belongings before taking my hand into his so that we could head out the hospital.

Jay

Instead of taking us home, I had Justin take me to our apartment that we'd use to lay low. While Justin drove, I ran down to him what went down when my phone fell out of my hand and I also told him that I felt like Tisha had something to do with it.

"For starters, the hoe keeps too many niggas at her house. Normally, if she knows somebody is coming through or even if she doesn't, she keeps her door unlocked so that a nigga can walk right in. She only locks her front door if she is in the midst of entertaining. She knew I was coming and had her door locked. Not only that, her previous visitor was still sitting out around the corner watching her house."

When I finished talking, he looked at me and then his eyes darted towards RiRi who was now sleeping. I looked at her to be sure she was still asleep before I continued. Lowering my voice, I said, "It was that nigga

Dre from Wilson Street Projects. He was sitting out there and then when I left I noticed some of his niggas following. I didn't know it was them at first until I saw that red Crown Vic with tha 26s on it following me too. Then, I saw Dre ass in traffic as well when the niggas in the Vic started shooting."

"So what's the plan?" Justin asked.

"We take out as many of them as we can. When Tisha gets out the hospital, I may play nice to get her to admit what she did and go from there. She was a little hurt that I chose RiRi over her," I told him just as we pulled up to Fairwind Apartments in North Charleston.

We got out of the car and I picked up RiRi to carry her into the apartment. I was still in a little pain but it wasn't too bad. I was glad we were on the first floor instead of the second, cause even though I wasn't in too much pain, baby got back!! That would've been a lot of ass to carry up the stairs. When we walked into the apartment, I walked to my room and laid RiRi across the bed and pulled off her shoes so that she could be comfortable. I then kissed her on the forehead and just watched her sleep.

After standing there for a few minutes, I walked out of the room shutting the door and walked in the living room with my brother who had already called up our crew. I walked in as he was filling them in on what had already transpired. One of the shooters we had spoke up and said, "Well, you right about it being Dre and nem. He done been through the hood talkin bout he took you out. Nobody really knows that you survived. Hopefully, Tisha keeps her mouth shut while she in the hospital. Word is ya girl fucked her up and they had to transfer her to MUSC for her injuries."

When he said that, I nodded and said, "Well, let them keep thinking it. We gone act like I'm on life support or worse. Do we have niggas monitoring her room?" I asked. He nodded his head yes. "Okay, well if y'all know where he at and what he got going on, then we move tonight," I said. From there, we mapped out a plan to take a course of action against Dre and his crew.

We sat up strategizing for a while and then I had one of my boys to go out and get some food for me and RiRi for when she woke up. I took it to the room so that I could wake her up to eat. When I walked in the room, RiRi was already awake and watching TV.
"How long you been up lil mama?" I asked her.
"Just really got up," she said while yawning.
"Okay, well just in time. I had one of my boys to come out and bring you back some food from Peking. I got you some General Tso's chicken with pork fried rice and egg roll," I told her. She smiled and said thanks. She dug into her food as I ate mine and we watched TV together. "So, you never told me that you was a mini Rambo," I said as she laughed.
"I mean, when bitches try me I tend to let it slide to an extent," she said. I laughed because I didn't know she was lethal with them hands. Once our laughter died down, all I could do is stare at her beauty. She saw me watching her and began to stare at me as well. We started to kiss the way we were kissing earlier before we were interrupted. I began to rub my hands across her body as I continued to kiss her. She started to moan and my dick began to harden at the thought of what I could do to her. The more she moaned and the deeper we kissed, the more I wanted to make love to her.

It took everything in me to pull away and to stop the kiss. As I pulled away, I just stared at her beauty as she opened her eyes and looked at me. "What's wrong?" she asked.

"Just sitting here mesmerized by your beauty," I told her with a smile.

She smiled back and said, "Well, why just be mesmerized," with a seductive look in her eyes. I looked at her and had to shake my head. She was just so damn beautiful and I didn't want to take advantage of her beauty or innocence. I stood up and put my hand over my dick so that I wouldn't offend her.

"What's wrong, did I do something wrong?" RiRi asked.

I shook my head and said, "Nah ma. You ain't did shit wrong. You doing everything right."

"So why'd you stop kissing me and why you standing up like you about to leave?" she asked as she stood to her feet as well and stepped towards me. I put my free hand over my face while the other continued to cover my imprint.

"Ri, baby, it ain't that I don't wanna make love to you. I do, but I don't want to take advantage of you or make you feel like I'm pressuring you. I know you got yo v-card and you tryna make sure that-"

She stopped me mid-sentence and said, "Well, how do you know I don't have my v-card?" she said.

I felt myself getting a little angry at the thought that someone else had taken that v-card before I could. She began to laugh, "I'm just kidding. I almost lost it once but it didn't work out well. But how do you know I'm not wanting to do it now," she said. She gave me a look that said that she was serious as a heart attack.

"Damn, girl you sure that's something that you wanna do?" I asked her. She nodded her head and kissed me again. For someone that was a virgin, she sure was bold. I stepped back towards the bed while kissing her and laid her gently across the bed as I continued to rub her body down. I slowly lifted her shirt after removing my own, and started to kiss down her neck and rub her breasts with one hand and her ass with the other. Her breasts were begging to be released from the bra that she had on. I kissed further down while still massaging her breasts and ass and then I removed her pants and underwear.

I stopped kissing her body and asked again, "You sure you wanna do this?" Instead of answering, RiRi pushed my head down as I started to make love to her with my tongue and finger. She continued to grab onto my head as she began to moan louder and louder. My tongue was working into overdrive as I continued to annihilate her pussy with it. She was screaming out my name as she suddenly began to shake.

"Jay, oh my God!! What is happening to me!! Oh! Ah!!" I smiled while I continued to move faster with both my tongue and finger. She continued to shake and then all of a sudden, all I could hear was splashing around as she came and began to squirt. I sat up and smiled since I had gotten her to squirt and cum for the first time ever. She thought she was gone off my tongue, wait till she had this 10-inch monster in her guts. I looked down at her as she covered her face like she was embarrassed.

"I can't believe I did that. And I think I peed in your bed," she said as I began to laugh at her.

"Nah, Ri baby, you good. What you had happen to you was an orgasm and you ended up squirting. Don't be ashamed, I have that kind of effect," I told her while removing her hands from her face. She swung at me like she was mad. I laughed again at her and then licked my lips. "Well, I'll go take a shower so that I can get him together," I told her while pointing at my dick.

"What do you mean? You don't want me anymore?" she asked with hurt evident in her face and voice.

"Nah, baby, it ain't even like that. I didn't want you to feel pressured into doing something that you ain't ready to do. I'm good. I'm no stranger to Palmala."

She scrunched up her face and said, "Palmala?"

I laughed and said, "Yeah." After I said that, I showed her what I meant, which was jacking my dick. She just shook her head and threw a pillow at me. I laughed and went into the bathroom that was in my bedroom. I turned the shower on hot instead of cold, because if my ass tried to just get it down with the cold water my blue balls would probably burst. I closed my eyes and slowly started to stroke my dick while imagining it was RiRi's pussy around it instead of my hand. I didn't want to cum yet because I needed this release, but the feeling of wanting her was so intense I knew I'd cum at any second. Suddenly, the bathroom door opened and she stood there in all of her naked glory.

"How about, instead of Palmala, you and Roneshia have some time together? I don't like to share," she said.

I cracked a smile and said, "Baby girl, I can wait. I ain't that hard up."

She laughed and said, "Well, your third leg says otherwise." I couldn't do anything but laugh at her as she walked closer and got into the shower with me. She began kissing me almost as hard as she was when we were in the bedroom.

"Baby, you know you ain't gotta do this right," I asked her.

"But I want to. Just make sure that I'm not giving this to you in vain," she said.

I nodded my head and continued to kiss her soft, full lips. I pulled her closer and kept on kissing on her being careful to not hurt her in the areas where she was injured by her father. I reached behind me and turned the water off in the shower while still kissing her and walked her back into the room while laying her down on my bed. I reached down to play with her wetness to get her ready for what was about to come. She winced a little but spread her legs wider. It was a tight fit for my fingers so I could only imagine how she'd react when I put my dick in her.

I grabbed my dick next and began to rub it up and down her clit with one hand making it wetter while squeezing her soft ass breasts with the other hand and still kissing her. She began to moan while I was playing in her wetness so I stopped kissing her and looked in her eyes and, as if she knew the answer to my question before I could ask, she nodded her head yes. I scooted back a little so that I could slowly ease my penis into her. As soon as I put the head in she tensed up and said, "Okay, keep going." I nodded and eased in some more. She began to whimper and I could tell she was in pain. I tried to pull out but she pulled me closer and urged me to keep going. I eased in some more until I could feel her hymen break and once that happened she let out a loud moan and screech.

I looked down and saw the tears in her eyes so I kissed them away as I began to slow stroke her. Even if it wasn't her first time, I'd have to slow stroke her ass because she was so tight. That shit felt like heaven. Everything just felt right about this, us. I had to keep taking deep breaths so that I wouldn't nut so fast. I started to speed up my pace while we both were moaning and she was looking me in the eyes. She was so beautiful and now that we were connected intimately, I needed her to know that she couldn't fuck nobody else.

"Damn, yo shit tight bae. You know you mine right?" I said to her.

She nodded her head as she continued to make her sex faces. Next thing I know it felt like she was tightening herself up more down there and I ain't had no choice but to let off in her. We both screamed out at the same time while she told me she loved me and I did the same. I knew then that I made the right choice by cutting Tisha's hoe ass off and making RiRi my baby.

As she laid in my arms, my eyes I got heavy. I kissed her forehead and said, "I love you girl and you fuck with me you stuck with me." She nodded and closed her eyes and a few seconds later I was asleep with my baby in my arms.

RiRi

That was so perfect and I was glad I lost my virginity to Jay instead of some random ass nigga. As bad as I wanted to go to sleep, I had shit to do. After about fifteen minutes of listening to Jay snore, I slipped out of the bed and went to the bathroom to shower which made me only want to sleep all the more. After I finished, I put on some of Jay's shorts and a tank top that I found in his room. I found a new toothbrush in his bathroom and brushed my teeth and then put on my shoes and grabbed my phone before peeking out the bedroom to see if Justin was anywhere close. When I didn't see him, I tiptoed out of the room and went to the living room while making sure I didn't see anyone else. I finally made it to the front door and slipped out the door into this hot Charleston night. I kept walking until I saw the car I was looking for. I went to the door and got in on the passenger side.

"Bitch, it took you long enough," Dominique said. I laughed at her as she gave me a once over. "Oh shit, you glowing and shit!! You finally done gave up the cooch!!" When she said that I laughed harder as she joined in.

"Bitch, cut it out and let's go," I told her. She nodded her head while still laughing and put the car in drive. We briefly talked while driving to our destination and sang to the songs that were playing on the radio.

We finally reached our destination while silence filled the car. "So you ready Ri?" Dominique asked.

"Hell, yeah. This bitch tried me and you know how I rock. I'll let the shit go temporarily but she was straight outta pocket today. And her friend gonna catch it too," I said.

Dominique nodded and we got out of her car. We were on the Eastside on America Street and that area stayed with some shit. Surprisingly, it ain't been too many mothafuckas out tonight. We headed to the apartment that we were told where we could find this bitch and she was in there talking all loud and ghetto with the back door open and just the screen door closed. Being that she was playing music around 11 at night, one might not think to listen to her conversation, but she piqued my interest when I heard her say Jay's name.

"Nigga I know what I said. But you said that all you was planning to do was rob his ass and then rough him up some. You ain't been supposed to kill him!!" she yelled through tears.

We then heard a male voice speaking and say, "Bitch, you knew what it was. When I come to you about getting some shit crackin you know what it was. Now, normally all I do is rob, but you the one call and say handle the shit and dats what tha fuck I did. He should've been more prepared."

"Dre, that shit ain't cool. When you stepped to me with this elaborate plan, you said, set him up to be robbed!! Not-"

Slap! Slap!

When we heard that, we knew she had got hit. Luckily, her little apartment was on the end and all we had to do was stand under the trees pretending we was with the people posted up near the building. We had our own liquor bottle that we was sipping from so we did that and pretended we were on our phones while discreetly listening. I looked up and noticed some nigga lookin at me like he knew me so I stared back and he turned his head. From time to time I could still feel him looking at me.

"Look, Tisha, you was with tha shits from the beginning so don't switch up on me now. Don't nobody know what's going on. He thought I was gone when he came to yo house and all I did was switch cars. I been waiting on you to let me know when you wanted to go through with the plan so I already had niggas on standby," the guy I now knew as Dre said.

"Yeah, okay, just make sure you have the rest of my money," Tisha said.

He laughed and said, "I got you as soon as I come back through to get my dick sucked tomorrow." I instantly gagged at what he said.

She laughed and told him, "I got you, just make sure you here before Eric come cause I'm fucking him and ain't gonna be ready to suck nobody else dick after fucking him."

He sucked his teeth and said, "I know you a hoe and all, but I ain't wanna hear about my homey dick. I only wanna hear you talk about mine." His voice got closer as he walked to the back door about to leave. She giggled and flipped him off as he walked up to some of the niggas hanging out and about near her apartment.

While he dapped them up, she stood on the porch smoking a blunt. As soon as she was done and went back in the house, we looked at each other and then followed behind her.

"Man, whoever this is, close my door and lock it!! Y'all know the deal, lock my shit so niggas can know I'm entertaining," she yelled from what I assume was her room. She was just making the shit too easy right about now. Dominique locked the door as I walked towards where I heard Tisha's voice come from. She was in the only bedroom in the apartment with her back turned towards me getting undressed. I walked in not even bothering to be silent as I walked in behind her. Not one to hate on the next chick, but she was cute or whatever not including the knots on her face and head from trying me at the hospital, with her Miami bought body.

I walked up to her and grabbed the back of her neck, turned her towards me and then proceeded to punch her in the face. When she caught on that I wasn't a nigga there to dig in what may have been left of her walls, she tried to fight back. I backed off just enough for her to get a good look at my face. She smiled and spit out some of the blood that was leaking from her mouth.

"So the little homeless bitch decided to come out and play? Well bitch you caught me off guard since I was checking on my man, but I'm finna sho yo ass that you ain't got shit on me," she said as she tried to rush me. As soon as she ran over towards me, I cracked her with a hard jab that sent her stumbling. She thought I fucked her up in the hospital, if only she knew that I was just having fun right about now. When she tried to charge again, I hit her with a two-piece that immediately knocked her out.

Dominique came into the room by then and laughed while she helped me to get the bitch dressed in some of her slutty clothes so that we could finish out with our plan. We then put some shades on her face since the fool really does wear sunglasses at night to go with her outfits. We then each took a hold of her arms and walked her out her front door since the niggas was hanging around the back. We walked out her door towards Dominique's car while laughing. The plan was supposed to pretend to laugh, but we were really laughing at how stupid this bitch was and how easy it was to get her out of here. We sat her in the backseat of the car as if she was so drunk and then Dominique got in the front seat while I got in back with Tisha in case she woke up. We headed to North Charleston off of Spruill Avenue to the shipyard where Domninque said they'd be to commence with our plan.

Jay

I was a little disappointed when I woke up to see that RiRi was gone. I was a little caught off guard that after losing her virginity to me that she would just haul ass on me like I was some hoe ass nigga out here. I was upset but I didn't have time to hit her up and see where she was, but I was definitely gonna do it after we finished handling business.

I went in my bathroom to shower and brush my teeth since I couldn't go anywhere without handling my hygiene. When I finished, I got dressed in what I called my ready to go outfit which consisted of an all-black polo tee, some black sweats and all black Timbs that I also used when it was time to stomp a nigga out. I walked out my room and saw Justin in the hall as if he was getting ready to knock on my room door to come get me.

"Glad to see you're ready," he said with a smirk on his face.

I laughed at him and said, "Nigga, I'm always ready."

"Okay, cool, well let's hurry up and get outta here before RiRi wake up and start looking for yo ass," he said.

I looked at the bed and then looked at him and said, "Man, she already gone."

He raised his eyebrows and said, "She gone already? Where she at? I thought for sure her ass would've been knocked out after I heard y'all in that room while I was tryna get me some."

He then started to laugh as I shook my head and said, "Shit, me too. I thought so, too, but I woke up and she done dipped out on me. I'm gonna holla at her about that after we handle this business."

He looked at me and laughed and said, "Damn bro, she straight dipped on yo ass." I shook my head and kept walking as we continued out the apartment.

I decided to change the subject as we headed to the car, "So, what's up with that info on Dre?"

As Justin started up the car he cracked a smile and said, "Oh, we got that nigga at the shipyard down the street from the Macon."

I smiled and said, "Shit, that's wassup then; let's go I'll handle this then." We headed to I-26 to go to the shipyard to handle Dre and whoever else was with him. While driving, Justin filled me in on how our homeboy Rasheed had overheard a conversation that Dre was having with Tisha and how she and him set me up to be robbed. As I sat and thought about it all I remembered seeing him in her house that day I went by to let her know that I wasn't gonna be fuckin with her on no sex tip no more.

"On another note, Rasheed said when they snatched Dre up from ole girl house RiRi was standing outside with her home girl on Tisha back porch. He did try to keep an eye on them but when he saw an opportunity he snatched Dre ass up so I don't know if them fighting at the hospital was a part of they plan or if she on some other shit," he said as my mind tried to process everything he said.

"The fuck she doing on the East Side? Ain't no way they working together cause Tisha didn't even know her and couldn't stand her. She was mad that I was finna wife up RiRi. Man, this shit is just too much," I said while pulling out my phone to call RiRi. Her phone went to voicemail and I called back two more times and it kept going to voicemail. I decided to shoot her a text to see where she was.

"Man, don't worry about shorty right now, we got some business to handle I need you to get your mind right," Justin said while passing me a blunt. I nodded my head cause he was right and we were approaching our destination. When we pulled up to the shipyard, we drove around to make sure that we weren't being followed and to make sure there was nobody lurking in the area like they did when I got ambushed leaving Tisha's house.

"When we done with this and I check on RiRi we need to hit that bitch Tisha up since she set us up," I told Justin.

"Already on it, I got somebody waiting on her to get back home cause one of her neighbors said she went out to the club with two of her homegirls and knows she'll probably be back by tomorrow evening, but if we can find out what club she in then we can have her snatched up and brought to us," he said.

"Well, I know she always goes to either Echelon or Fantasies and both of em on Ashley Phosphate so tell them to scope out those two," I told him.

He said okay and pulled out his phone to text whoever he had on it. After we checked out the scene, Justin parked in front of one of the buildings that we normally handled situations in since the supervisor for this particular area would have us handle his situations as well. We walked inside and saw where they had Dre tied up and his homeboy Eric was next to him as well getting his ass beat by a couple of my goons. Since the rest of the niggas that was with him shootin at me had gotten fucked up in that car accident, it was just him, Eric, and Tisha left to deal with. I walked in with a smile on my face, as Dre looked up at me with blood leaking from his eye.

"Dre, my nigga, what's good," I said.

He looked at me and shook his head, "Man, fuck whatchu talkin bout, just kill me pussy ass nigga!" I laughed at him trying to be tough when I could clearly see the pain in his eyes.

I kneeled down so that I could be in eye contact with him and said, "You sure about that." When he spit his blood in my face I lost it. One thing I couldn't stand was a mothafucka that would spit. That was some of the nastiest shit ever and real way to make me kill a mothafucka. I commenced to whipping his ass while he was in the chair. I then decided to untie him from the chair to see if he would fight back and he just laid there like the pussy he was.

My brother had already started to put in work on Eric who decided that he wanted to talk, "Man chill man. All that was supposed to happen was we rob you since you came in our hood and was making more bread than a lil bit. When we tried to get down with you, you acted like it wasn't possible so when Dre had the idea to just try and take you out I was down with it. It was easier once you made Tisha mad and she decided to work with us," he said.

I looked at him and said, "Well, when you stepped to me about making moves to be on the team you started running yo mouth about who ran what and how to get them out the way. It was informative, but that showed me that you can't be trusted. Just like now, you snitching out the whys and the parties involved with shooting at me. You can't be trusted." As soon as I finished my sentence Justin pulled out his gun and stuck it in Eric's mouth and pulled the trigger.

As soon as he did that I heard clapping and turned my head with my gun drawn while the rest of my crew did the same. When I saw who it was I lowered my gun.

"Well, don't make us miss all the fun," RiRi said while she was dragging Tisha in with her friend Dominique behind her with a gun to Tisha's head.

"What the fuck Ri? What y'all doing here?" I asked. She just laughed as she snatched Tisha forward and threw her to the floor.

"Jay, baby, help me! You just gonna let this homeless bitch do this to me?" Tisha exclaimed.

RiRi kicked her in the face and said, "Baby? Bitch you are bolder than I thought. You'd think with a gun to yo head that you'd shut the fuck up but you still throwing insults. I bet baby won't think nothing more of you when he finds out you set him up to get shot at. See, initially I came to your house to fuck you up for the disrespect at the hospital and overheard your name in a conversation. And when I knocked yo ass out at the hospital I saw you texting Dre," and she motioned her head in Dre's direction, "and when I saw that I knew I had to come see about you. Then y'all had the balls to be on the projects talking about it with the door wide open. Bitch, how dumb are you?" she said as she delivered another kick to Tisha's already bruised face.

Next thing I knew the nigga Dre tried to rush me. He caught me off guard but I caught my footing and started to put that work on him. He started to lose his breath seeing as though he was already fucked up to begin with.

"Aye, bruh calm down, we about to end this," Justin said as he grabbed my arm. I looked at him at him and nodded my head as I backed up from my handy work. I grabbed my gun as Justin dragged Dre's body next to Tisha's. I was in awe at how RiRi came through for me but we would have to talk about her handling business after this. All of a sudden Dre started to laugh as if he wasn't about to die so I looked at him to see what he was laughing at.

"What's so funny fuck boy?" I asked him.

He continued to laugh and cough up blood before saying, "You are. You so damn smart till you stupid," he said as he continued to laugh. I looked at Justin as he shrugged his shoulders. "Shit be right in your face and you still blind. Ain't that right Justin?" He said as he laughed again. I looked at Justin confused as he gave me the same look.

"Nigga, don't do that; you said you ready to die so die," Justin said before filling both Dre and Tisha with bullets.

Made in the USA
Columbia, SC
16 November 2021

49060762R00037